THE SANTA CLAUS BOOK

By Eileen Daly

Illustrated by
Florence Sarah Winship

A GOLDEN BOOK • NEW YORK

Western Publishing Company, Inc.
Racine, Wisconsin 53404

Santa's sleigh was piled high with toys. And Santa's list of boys and girls was so long that it made a curly tail behind the sleigh.

"Ho-ho!" laughed Santa as the sleigh landed softly on a rooftop. "This *is* a good Christmas!"

Down the chimney he went. He put a doll under the Christmas tree and a yellow truck beside the doll.

At John's house, he left a train. And he put a surprise in the red caboose.

"The next house is Davy's," Santa said as he sailed across the sky.

He placed a soft teddy bear beside Davy's pillow. Santa's elves had made the small bear just for Davy.

"The next house is Davy's," Santa said as he sailed across the sky.

He placed a soft teddy bear beside Davy's pillow. Santa's elves had made the small bear just for Davy.

He left a jumping jack for Sally and a drum for Billy. Then he checked his long list to see who was next.

As he read, he felt something tugging at the end of the list.

A little lost puppy was chewing Santa's list!

"Ho-ho!" said Santa. "You're a hungry fellow!
We will have to find a home for you."

Santa tucked the puppy into his sack. He put him right on top of a furry toy tiger.

At Jimmy's house, Santa looked around. Did the puppy belong to Jimmy? No. Jimmy had two little kittens.

Did the puppy belong to Jodi? No. Jodi had a pretty parakeet.

Then Santa came to Mike's house. Pinned to Mike's Christmas stocking was a note:

"Well, well," said Santa. He opened his sack to get his little lost friend. But where was the little puppy?

Santa looked under the toy boats in his sack.
No puppy there.

He looked under the toy guitars. No puppy there, either.

Then Santa looked inside a dollhouse. And there was the puppy, sound asleep.

Santa put the puppy in Mike's stocking. He tied a ribbon around it to hold the puppy snugly.

Then he tiptoed into Mike's room and put the sock full of puppy beside Mike's pillow.

When Mike woke up and found his puppy, my,
he was happy! So was the puppy.

And jolly old Santa Claus was the happiest of all as he called back, "Merry Christmas, Mike. Merry Christmas, EVERYONE!"